CHRISTOPHER ROBIN
AND POOH COME TO
AN ENCHANTED
PLACE

CHRISTOPHER ROBIN
AND POOH COME TO
AN ENCHANTED
PLACE

A. A. MILNE

illustrated by
ERNEST H. SHEPARD

CHRISTOPHER ROBIN
AND POOH COME TO
AN ENCHANTED
PLACE

Christopher Robin was going away.
Nobody knew why he was going; nobody
knew where he was going; indeed,
nobody even knew why he knew that
Christopher Robin *was* going away. But
somehow or other everybody in the
Forest felt that it was happening at last.
Even Smallest-of-all, a friend-and-
relation of Rabbit's who thought he had
once seen Christopher Robin's foot, but

couldn't be quite sure because perhaps it was something else, even S. of A. told himself that Things were going to be Different; and Late and Early, two other friends-and-relations, said, 'Well, Early?' and 'Well, Late?' to each other in such a hopeless sort of way that it really didn't seem any good waiting for the answer.

One day when he felt that he couldn't wait any longer, Rabbit brained out a Notice, and this is what it said:

'Notice a meeting of everybody will meet at the House at Pooh Corner to pass a Rissolution By Order Keep to the Left Signed Rabbit.'

He had to write this out two or three times before he could get the rissolution to look like what he thought it was going to when he began to spell it; but, when at last it was finished, he took it round to everybody and read it out to them. And they all said they would come.

'Well,' said Eeyore that afternoon, when he saw them all walking up to his house, 'this *is* a surprise. Am *I* asked too?'

'Don't mind Eeyore,' whispered Rabbit to Pooh. 'I told him all about it this morning.'

Everybody said 'How-do-you-do' to Eeyore, and Eeyore said that he didn't, not to notice, and then they sat down; and as soon as they were all sitting down, Rabbit stood up again.

'We all know why we're here,' he said, 'but I have asked my friend Eeyore —'

'That's Me,' said Eeyore. 'Grand.'

'I have asked him to Propose a
Rissolution.' And he sat down again. 'Now
then, Eeyore,' he said.

'Don't Bustle me,' said Eeyore, getting
up slowly. 'Don't now-then me.' He took
a piece of paper from behind his ear, and
unfolded it. 'Nobody knows anything
about this,' he went on. 'This is a
Surprise.' He coughed in an important
way, and began again: 'What-nots and
Etceteras, before I begin, or perhaps I

should say, before I end, I have a piece of Poetry to read to you. Hitherto — hitherto — a long word meaning — well, you'll see what it means directly — hitherto, as I was saying, all the Poetry in the Forest has been written by Pooh, a Bear with a Pleasing Manner but a Positively Startling Lack of Brain. The Poem which I am now about to read to you was written by Eeyore, or Myself, in a Quiet Moment. If somebody will take Roo's bull's eye away from him, and wake up Owl, we shall all be able to enjoy it.

I call it — POEM.'

This was it:

Christopher Robin is going.
At least I think he is.
Where
Nobody knows.
But he is going —
I mean he goes
(To rhyme with 'knows')
Do we care?
(To rhyme with 'where')
We do
Very much.
*(I haven't got a rhyme for that
    'is' in the second line yet.*
Bother.)
*(Now I haven't got a rhyme for
    bother. Bother.)*
Those two bothers will have
    to rhyme with each other
Buther.
The fact is this is more difficult
    than I thought,
I ought —
(Very good indeed)
I ought
To begin again,
But it is easier
To stop.

Christopher Robin, good-bye,
I
(Good)
I
And all your friends
Sends —
I mean all your friend
Send —
(Very awkward this, it keeps going wrong.)
Well, anyhow, we send
Our love
END.

'If anybody wants to clap,' said Eeyore when he had read this, 'now is the time to do it.'

They all clapped.

'Thank you,' said Eeyore. 'Unexpected and gratifying, if a little lacking in Smack.'

'It's much better than mine,' said Pooh admiringly, and he really thought it was.

'Well,' explained Eeyore modestly, 'it was meant to be.'

'The rissolution,' said Rabbit, 'is that we all sign it, and take it to Christopher Robin.'

So it was signed PooH,

WOL,

PIGLET,

EOR,

RABBIT,

KANGA,

BLOT,

SMUDGE,

and they all went off to Christopher
Robin's house with it.

'Hallo, everybody,' said Christopher
Robin — 'Hallo, Pooh.'

They all said 'Hallo,' and felt awkward
and unhappy suddenly, because it was a
sort of good-bye they were saying, and
they didn't want to think about it. So they

stood around, and waited for somebody else to speak, and they nudged each other, and said 'Go on,' and gradually Eeyore was nudged to the front, and the others crowded behind him.

'What is it, Eeyore?' asked Christopher Robin.

Eeyore swished his tail from side to side, so as to encourage himself, and began.

'Christopher Robin,' he said, 'we've come to say — to give you — it's called — written by — but we've all — because we've heard, I mean we all know — well, you see, it's — we — you — well, that, to put it as shortly as possible, is what it is.' He turned round angrily on the others and said, 'Everybody crowds round so in this Forest. There's no Space. I never saw a more Spreading lot of animals in my life, and all in the wrong places. Can't you *see* that Christopher Robin wants to be alone? I'm going.' And he humped off.

Not quite knowing why, the others began edging away, and when Christopher Robin had finished reading POEM, and was looking up to say 'Thank you,' only Pooh was left.

'It's a comforting sort of thing to have,' said Christopher Robin, folding up the paper, and putting it in his pocket. 'Come on, Pooh,' and he walked off quickly.

'Where are we going?' said Pooh, hurrying after him, and wondering whether it was to be an Explore or a What-shall-I-do-about-you-know-what.

'Nowhere,' said Christopher Robin.

So they began going there, and after they had walked a little way Christopher Robin said:

'What do you like doing best in the world, Pooh?'

'Well,' said Pooh, 'what I like best —' and then he had to stop and think. Because although Eating Honey *was* a very good thing to do, there was a moment just before you began to eat it which was better than when you were, but he didn't know what it was called. And then he thought that being with Christopher Robin was a very good thing to do, and having Piglet near was a very friendly thing to have; and so, when he had thought it all out, he said, 'What I like best in the whole world is Me and Piglet going to see You, and You saying, "What about a little something?" and Me saying, "Well, I shouldn't mind a little something, should you, Piglet," and it being a hummy sort of day outside, and birds singing.'

'I like that too,' said Christopher Robin, but what I like *doing* best is Nothing.'

'How do you do Nothing?' asked Pooh, after he had wondered for a long time.

'Well, it's when people call out at you just as you're going off to do it, "What are you going to do, Christopher Robin?" and

you say,"Oh, nothing," and then you go
and do it.'

'Oh, I see,' said Pooh.

'This is a nothing sort of thing that
we're doing now.'

'Oh, I see,' said Pooh again.

'It means just going along, listening to
all the things you can't hear, and not
bothering.'

'Oh!' said Pooh.

They walked on, thinking of This and
That, and by-and-by they came to an
enchanted place on the very top of the
Forest called Galleons Lap, which is sixty-
something trees in a circle; and
Christopher Robin knew that it was
enchanted because nobody had ever been
able to count whether it was sixty-three or
sixty-four, not even when he tied a piece
of string round each tree after he had
counted it. Being enchanted, its floor was
not like the floor of the Forest, gorse and

bracken and heather, but close-set grass, quiet and smooth and green. It was the only place in the Forest where you could sit down carelessly, without getting up again almost at once and looking for somewhere else. Sitting there they could see the whole world spread out until it reached the sky, and whatever there was all the world over was with them in Galleons Lap.

Suddenly Christopher Robin began to tell Pooh about some of the things: People called Kings and Queens and something called Factors, and a place called Europe, and an island in the middle of the sea where no ships came, and how you make a Suction Pump (if you want to), and when Knights were Knighted, and what comes from Brazil. And Pooh, his back against one of the sixty-something trees, and his paws folded in front of him, said 'Oh!' and 'I don't know,' and thought

how wonderful it would be to have a Real
Brain which could tell you things. And
by-and-by Christopher Robin came to an
end of the things, and was silent, and he
sat there looking out over the world, and
wishing it wouldn't stop.

But Pooh was thinking too, and he said
suddenly to Christopher Robin:

'Is it a very Grand thing to be an
Afternoon, what you said?'

'A what?' said Christopher Robin lazily, as he listened to something else.

'On a horse?' explained Pooh.

'A Knight?'

'Oh, was that it?' said Pooh. 'I thought it was a — Is it as Grand as a King and Factors and all the other things you said?'

'Well, it's not as grand as a King,' said Christopher Robin, and then, as Pooh seemed disappointed, he added quickly, 'but it's grander than Factors.'

'Could a Bear be one?'

'Of course he could!' said Christopher Robin. 'I'll make you one.' And he took a stick and touched Pooh on the shoulder, and said, 'Rise, Sir Pooh de Bear, most faithful of all my Knights.'

So Pooh rose and sat down and said 'Thank you,' which is the proper thing to say when you have been made a Knight, and he went into a dream again, in which he and Sir Pump and Sir Brazil and

Factors lived together with a horse, and
were faithful Knights (all except Factors,
who looked after the horse) to Good King
Christopher Robin . . . and every now
and then he shook his head, and said to
himself, 'I'm not getting it right.' Then
he began to think of all the things
Christopher Robin would want to tell him
when he came back from wherever he was
going to, and how muddling it would be

for a Bear of Very Little Brain to try and get them right in his mind. 'So, perhaps,' he said sadly to himself, 'Christopher Robin won't tell me any more,' and he wondered if being a Faithful Knight meant that you just went on being faithful without being told things.

Then, suddenly again, Christopher Robin, who was still looking at the world with his chin in his hands, called out 'Pooh!'

'Yes?' said Pooh.

'When I'm — when — Pooh!'

'Yes, Christopher Robin?'

'I'm not going to do Nothing any more.'

'Never again?'

'Well, not so much. They don't let you.'

Pooh waited for him to go on, but he was silent again.

'Yes, Christopher Robin?' said Pooh helpfully.

'Pooh, when I'm — *you* know — when I'm *not* doing Nothing, will you come up here sometimes?'

'Just Me?'

'Yes, Pooh.'

'Will you be here too?'

'Yes, Pooh, I will be really. I *promise* I will be, Pooh.'

'That's good,' said Pooh.

'Pooh, *promise* you won't forget about me, ever. Not even when I'm a hundred.'

Pooh thought for a little.

'How old shall *I* be then?'

'Ninety-nine.'

Pooh nodded.

'I promise,' he said.

Still with his eyes on the world Christopher Robin put out a hand and felt for Pooh's paw.

'Pooh,' said Christopher Robin earnestly, 'if I — if I'm not quite —' he stopped and tried again — 'Pooh, *whatever* happens, you *will* understand, won't you?'

'Understand what?'

'Oh, nothing.' He laughed and jumped to his feet. 'Come on!'

'Where?' said Pooh.

'Anywhere,' said Christopher Robin.

So they went off together. But wherever they go, and whatever happens to them on the way, in that enchanted place on the top of the Forest a little boy and his Bear will always be playing.

Christopher Robin and Pooh Come to an Enchanted Place
is taken from *The House at Pooh Corner*
originally published in
Great Britain 11 October 1928
by Methuen & Co. Ltd
Text by A.A. Milne and line drawings by Ernest H. Shepard
copyright under the Berne Convention

This book club edition published by Grolier 1995
Published by arrangement with Reed Children's Books

First published in this edition 1991
by Methuen Children's Books
an imprint of Reed Children's Books
Michelin House, 81 Fulham Road, London SW3 6RB
and Auckland, Melbourne, Singapore and Toronto
Reprinted 1992, 1994, 1995

Printed in Hong Kong

ISBN 0 416 17202 4